G

BUSTER'S
blustery day

By Hisako Madokoro   English text by Patricia Lantier   Illustrated by Ken Kuroi

**For a free color catalog describing Gareth Stevens' list of high-quality books, call
1-800-542-2595 (USA) or 1-800-461-9120 (Canada). Gareth Stevens' Fax: (414) 225-0377.**

Library of Congress Cataloging-in-Publication Data

Madokoro, Hisako, 1938-
  [Kaze no hi no Korowan. English]
  Buster's blustery day / text by Hisako Madokoro ;
illustrations by Ken Kuroi.
      p.   cm. — (The Adventures of Buster the puppy)
  Translation of: Kaze no hi no Korowan.
  Summary: Buster is frightened by the strong winds
outside his dog house until he goes outside to play and
discovers what fun the wind can be.
  ISBN 0-8368-0494-5 (lib. bdg.)
  ISBN 0-8368-1265-4 (trade)
  [1. Winds—Fiction. 2. Dogs—Fiction.] I. Kuroi,
Ken, ill. II. Title. III. Series: Madokoro, Hisako, 1938-
Korowan. English.
PZ7.M2657Bue   1991
[E]—dc20   90-47927

North American edition first published in 1991 by
Gareth Stevens Publishing
1555 North RiverCenter Drive, Suite 201
Milwaukee, Wisconsin 53212, USA

This U.S. edition © 1991. Text © 1991 by Gareth
Stevens, Inc. First published as *Kaze No Hi No
Korowan* (*Korowan in the Wind*) in Japan with an
original © 1987 by Hisako Madokoro (text) and
Ken Kuroi (illustrations). English translation rights
arranged with CHILD HONSHA through Japan
Foreign-Rights Centre.

Cover design: Kristi Ludwig

Printed in the United States of America

4 5 6 7 8 9 98 97 96 95 94

Gareth Stevens Publishing
MILWAUKEE

"Mommy, I'm scared
of this loud noise,"
whimpered Buster.
"The walls are shaking!"

"Don't worry," said Buster's
mother. "It's just Mr. Wind."

3

4

After a while, Buster felt
braver and went out to play.
The grass swayed swiftly
from left to right, and the
leaves flew high up to
the sky.

5

Fluffy white clouds bumped
into each other as they raced
across the sky.

"I wish I could fly like that!"

Buster lay flat on his stomach
and pretended to be a cloud.

"Hold on, Mr. Ant! Mr. Wind
might carry you away!"

9

"Oh, yuk!" complained Buster. "I've got sand in my mouth." The tiny grains tickled his nose and eyes and ears.

Whoosh! The wind carried
the leaves away — high,
high, high into the sky.

"Please let me play," Buster
begged the leaves. "I'll run
as fast as you can fly."

"Wheee! Racing is fun!"

Buster played happily with the leaves as they swirled in the wind.

15

The leaves fell together
under a big tree.

Buster kicked through the
pile, scattering brown and
gold leaves everywhere.

17

"Hey! Cut it out!
Stop kicking the leaves
away!" croaked a tiny frog
hiding in the pile.

19

"Please let me sleep,"
grumbled the frog. "Mr. Wind
has made such a nice, soft
bed for me."

Buster helped the little frog get his bed back. He gathered more and more leaves for the pile.

"Sleep well, Froggy!"

23

Buster ran home. All this
play had made him hungry.

"Good night, Mr. Wind!
I had a great time today!"

24